MW01045128

TOUGH GUY

SUSANNAH BRIN

Artesian **Press**

P.O. Box 355, Buena Park, CA 90621

Take Ten Books
Thrillers

Bronco Buster	1-58659-041-3
Audio Cassette	1-58659-046-4
Audio CD	1-58659-325-0
The Climb	1-58659-042-1
Audio Cassette	1-58659-047-2
Audio CD	1-58659-326-9
Search and Rescue	1-58659-043-X
Audio Cassette	1-58659-048-0
Audio CD	1-58659-327-7
Timber	1-58659-044-8
Audio Cassette	1-58659-049-9
Audio CD	1-58659-328-5
Tough Guy	**1-58659-045-6**
Audio Cassette	**1-58659-050-2**
Audio CD	**1-58659-329-3**

Other Take Ten Themes:

Mystery	**Sports**	**Adventure**
Chillers	**Fantasy**	**Horror**
Disaster	**Romance**	

Development & Production: Laurel Associates, Inc.
Editor: Molly Mraz
Cover Illustrator:Fujiko
Graphic Design: Tony Amaro
©2004 Artesian Press

www.artesianpress.com

ISBN 1-58659-045-6

CONTENTS

Chapter 1 5

Chapter 2 14

Chapter 3 21

Chapter 4 28

Chapter 5 37

Chapter 6 45

Chapter 7 51

Chapter 8 56

Chapter 1

Joe Beesom heard the roar of the Harley-Davidson before he saw it. Against his back, he could feel the ground shudder as the giant bike stopped just inches from his outstretched legs. Joe slid out from under the old car he was working on and looked up.

There stood a middle-aged man with his hair cut short, military-style. His steely blue eyes stared down at Joe accusingly.

Joe scrambled to his feet. He noticed the man was wearing combat fatigues. Odd. And why was his leather jacket covered with medals? But many of the people in this one-horse town were weird. Except Joe's cousin Smitty.

Good old Smitty, Joe had decided, was cool—even though he acted like a hick. Smitty was funny and good-natured. And he usually let Joe take the lead, which he did as much as possible. They were both seventeen, but Joe liked to think of himself as better qualified to be the leader. After all, he was the one with street smarts.

There were a few other differences between the cousins, too. Smitty was taller and thinner. Joe was bolder and more confident. Sometimes Joe thought the only adventures that Smitty really enjoyed were the ones in the pages of his books.

"What do you think you're doing, man?" Joe cried out angrily. He was going to say more, but something in the way the older man looked at him made him stop.

"You get that part I ordered?" the man barked rudely.

Heading out toward the front of the

station, Joe could see Smitty leaning on a gas pump, reading a paperback. Behind him, he heard the revving of the Harley's engine as the man backed it out of the mechanic's bay.

"Hey, Smitty! Did we get the General's part in yet?" Joe yelled.

"What'd you call me, boy?" snarled the older man, coasting his bike toward where Joe stood.

"Nothing, mister. I didn't call you anything," said Joe. He ducked his head and rolled his eyes at his cousin.

Smitty threw Joe a warning glance. Then he turned to the man on the bike and smiled. "Your part didn't come in yet, Mr. Johnson. Dad said it should be here any day now."

"Yeah, that's what you said last time. You know, I've gotten supplies in the middle of the jungle faster than this. Your daddy should carry a bigger inventory," growled Johnson.

"Well, Mr. Johnson, we're just a

small station in a small town. But I'm sure we'll have that part this week," said Smitty. It bugged Joe to hear the note of apology in his cousin's voice.

"I'll be back," the scowling man said sternly. Glancing around as though he were sizing up enemy territory, he pointed to the side of the gas station where a brand-new Yamaha was parked. "Whose bike?"

Joe beamed with pride. For the moment he forgot his dislike of the man. "Mine! And let me tell you, it's a real mean machine."

The man on the Harley laughed. "Oh, yeah? It looks like a girl's bike to me." Then, gunning his bike, he drove off down the one-lane road and left the two young men in a cloud of dust. Smitty and Joe watched until the bike was just a black dot in the distance.

"Where does he get off calling my Yamaha a girl's bike? I should have slapped him upside the head for saying such a thing," said Joe, smarting from Johnson's insult.

"Forget it. Johnson's got a screw loose," said Smitty.

"You can say that again. What's he think he is—some kind of commando or something?" asked Joe.

"Who knows? They say he has a stockpile of weapons in his house, and that he's planted mines and booby traps all over his property."

"Wow, that *is* weird. What's he afraid of? World War III?" asked Joe.

"Look, I don't know. I just know that he's a mean, tough guy. Nobody around here messes with him. And you shouldn't call him the General," said Smitty. He looked back down at the book in his hand.

Joe took two little steps and faked a right jab at his cousin's book. "He isn't so tough. I bet I could take him." Dancing on his toes like a boxer, he turned toward the station window and boxed at his reflection in the glass.

I may be short, he thought to himself, *but I'm fast.* He spun back to face his cousin and playfully punched him in the stomach with a one-two combination. "Cut it out!" laughed Smitty, stepping away from his cousin.

Joe danced closer, feinting first with a right, then with a left hook. "I'm not scared of the General, Smitty. There were tougher guys than him in my high school," Joe bragged.

"Okay, okay. You're tougher than Johnson. Now will you let me finish my book? I'm right in the middle of a really good part," Smitty said as he ducked a punch.

An old blue pickup pulled into the station and parked near the mechanic's bay. A tall, thin, older man in bib overalls and a blue workshirt climbed out. Slamming the truck door, he walked toward them, carrying several brown paper packages. "I see you boys are hard at work as usual," the man teased. Then he placed the packages on top of the old red soda cooler that sat next to the station door.

"Hi, Dad," said Smitty. "Did anything come from the college?"

"Nope. But we got those new fan belts I ordered a month ago. And let's see—there's a water pump for Mrs. Simpson's Chevy, and here's Mr. Johnson's cycle part."

"Johnson was here just a few minutes ago asking about that part," said Smitty.

"Too bad I missed him. He's been waiting a long time for it to get here. I had to special-order it from back east," said Mr. Carpenter.

"We could take it out to him after we get off work," Joe offered. He picked up the small package containing the cycle part and studied it.

"No, we don't do house calls out here, Joe," laughed Mr. Carpenter.

"I know. But it seemed like he *really* wanted this part," said Joe, staring off in the direction Johnson had gone.

"He'll be back," said Mr. Carpenter.

"I just thought we could . . ."

Mr. Carpenter interrupted Joe before he could finish his sentence. "Get into a lot of trouble, if you ask me. Listen up, Joe! Stay clear of Johnson—and stay away from his place, too. He's as crazy as an old hoot owl."

"Joe's just upset because Johnson called his Yamaha a girl's bike," teased Smitty.

Mr. Carpenter glanced sharply at Smitty and then at Joe. "Don't pay it no mind. Like I said, he's crazy. Smitty, your mama and I are going over to your sister's house for the weekend. There's food in the fridge," he said, walking back to his truck. He opened the cab's door, then turned back to them. "You boys close up around six, now. And don't even think about bothering that crazy Johnson."

Joe waved good-bye to Mr. Carpenter, then looked down at the package in his hand. An idea was growing in his head that made him smile. He turned to his cousin. "Smitty, I been thinking."

"That's unusual," teased Smitty, his eyes dancing with amusement.

"Very funny," said Joe. "Anyway, I want to take my bike out and test that valve I replaced on it. Wanna come?"

"Sure," said Smitty.

Joe smiled to himself as he dropped the small package containing Johnson's cycle part into the pocket of his workshirt.

Chapter 2

"Come on, man. I told you I already locked the garage doors!" Joe yelled, impatiently revving up the engine on his bike. He wanted to get going.

Smitty glanced around the station one last time. Then he climbed on the bike behind Joe. "Okay, hit it!"

Joe gunned the engine and released the clutch. The bike surged forward like a racehorse leaving the gate. He headed toward the mountains in the same direction Johnson had taken earlier. As he sped along, Joe leaned forward, the wind whipping back his hair. He grinned and yelled over his shoulder, "Too fast for you, cuz?"

"Ha! I could *walk* faster than this!" Smitty yelled back.

"Oh, yeah? Well, hold onto your jeans." Joe twisted down on the hand throttle, forcing the bike to go faster and faster. The countryside flew by as they raced after the sun, which was slowly disappearing behind the mountains. "Yahoo!" Joe whooped.

He was happy. He loved this bike. It was part of the reason he'd agreed to spend his last summer before college working for his uncle. Only three more payments and he'd own the Yamaha free and clear.

They had the road to themselves. Occasionally a car or truck would pass them going in the opposite direction. But for the most part, they were alone. The narrow road cut straight into the mountain's foothills.

Joe turned his head sideways and yelled back to Smitty, "Exactly where does the General live?"

"Forget it!" Smitty shouted back.

But Joe didn't want to forget it. He

hit the brakes, and the bike screeched to a stop on the shoulder of the road. Turning to face Smitty, he reached into his shirt pocket and pulled out the package. "Look here. This is Johnson's bike part. As long as we're out here, we might as well drop it off."

Smitty's eyebrows knit together in one long frown line.

"I thought we were taking this ride to test out your new valve," he said.

"That, too," said Joe, grinning. "Look, Smitty, what's the harm in just dropping it off?" He stared straight into his cousin's blue eyes, challenging him to disagree.

"I don't know. Johnson's a strange one—*real* strange," said Smitty, glancing toward the mountains. "People out here don't like unexpected visitors. They really like to protect their privacy, if you know what I mean."

"We aren't visitors. We're making a delivery. Let's just drop off the part and go. Didn't you notice how bad the guy wanted this part?"

"Yeah, but . . ."

"So we're doing him a favor. He isn't going to get upset because we did him a favor, is he?" argued Joe.

"No, I guess not, but . . ."

Joe cut in before Smitty could think of another objection. "He's going to *thank* us for taking the time to drive the part out here. Come on, Smitty, lighten up. What do you say?"

Smitty didn't answer right away. He chewed on the corner of his bottom lip and stared off into space. Finally, he looked at Joe and said, "Okay. But as soon as we give him the part, we split right away."

"Right!" Joe grinned. He had known that his cousin would agree once they were this close to Johnson's place. "So where's his house?"

Smitty leaned forward and pointed. "See where the road forks to the right and disappears into the forest? It's at the end of that road."

Joe twisted the gas throttle a couple of times. The back wheel spun and kicked up loose dirt and rocks as it leapt forward. As they made the turn, clouds of dust rose in the air like smoke signals. "You think the General can see us coming?" yelled Joe.

"How could he miss us? I just hope he doesn't welcome us with a twenty-one-gun salute," answered Smitty.

Halfway up the mountain, they came to a clearing in the woods. At the top of the clearing stood an old wooden house with a wide porch. A barbed wire fence circled the perimeter of the property. Joe inched the bike forward to a wooden gate. Concertina wire lay curled across the top of the fence like an unraveled Slinky toy. A sign painted with a skull read *Keep Out.*

Smitty scanned the treeline on either side of the road. He couldn't see anything except the trees and brush. Everything was growing dark with the coming of night. "Maybe we should just tie the package to the gate and leave," suggested Smitty.

"No, he might not see it there," said Joe. He glanced around nervously. The place *was* spooky—the thick trees, the clearing, the concertina wire. Then he straightened his shoulders and bit back his own uneasiness. "Open the gate, will ya?" he yelled.

Smitty climbed off the bike and walked slowly toward the gate. An open padlock hung on the latch. Smitty pushed the gate inward so Joe could drive into the yard. "I don't see any lights on in the house," said Smitty as he climbed back onto the bike. "Maybe he isn't home."

Joe was hoping the same thing, but he didn't want Smitty to know that. He parked the bike in the side yard and saw an old barn behind the house. The doors of the barn were hanging open.

Joe knocked lightly on the front door of the house, but there was no answer. He glanced at Smitty and knocked again—harder this time. The door swung open. Leaning into the doorway, he called out, "Mr. Johnson! Hey, Mr. Johnson! Anybody home?"

The living room was empty and uninviting. He looked down a dark hallway and saw light under a door at the back of the house. As he started down the hall toward the light, Smitty grabbed his arm.

"Let's get out of here! We shouldn't be walking around in Johnson's house like this." Joe was surprised to see so much fear in Smitty's eyes.

Chapter 3

Joe angrily shook free of Smitty's grasp. "Will you quit worrying? He probably didn't hear me." Again, he called out, "Mr. Johnson! We've brought your cycle part." But again, silence.

"He's not here. Come on. Let's get out of here before he gets back," urged Smitty. He nervously looked back over his shoulder.

Joe didn't say anything. He hadn't come this far to turn back now. *And besides*, he thought to himself, *if Johnson caught us running out of the house now, he'd wonder what we've been up to.*

The old hardwood floor creaked under their weight as they crept down the dark hall. Then Joe thought he heard something. But the sound was only the loud humming of the old refrigerator.

"This is *crazy*, man," whispered Smitty as he followed Joe into the kitchen. His voice sounded breathless and panicky.

Joe tossed his head and laughed. "Chill out, Smitty, or you'll give yourself a heart attack." He didn't want Smitty to know that his own heart was pounding like a jackhammer.

A semicircle of light radiated from the crack under the door at the end of the hall. Joe knocked and called out, but no one answered. When he turned the doorknob, more light spilled into the kitchen. A naked light bulb illuminated narrow wooden stairs leading down into a basement. Halfway down the stairs, he let out a yell of surprise. "Whoa!" He looked up the stairs at his cousin. "Come here, Smitty! You gotta see this!"

Continuing down the stairs, Joe

smiled to himself when he heard Smitty coming after him. Curiosity was something that both boys definitely had in common.

"Look at this room!" exclaimed Smitty. "It's like a *museum*!" The walls were crowded with framed black-and-white photos of soldiers in action. Gold-framed shadow boxes with velvet backing displayed military medals, decorations, and insignias. A clothes rack sagged under the weight of several old military uniforms. A cavalry sword dangled at the end of the rack, its gold tassel shining in the light.

"Can you *believe* it?" said Joe, sounding like a child turned loose in a candy store. An assortment of weapons lay on a long wooden table. Each knife and gun was clean and highly polished. Joe picked up a gleaming rifle and aimed it at the stairs.

"I don't know if it's a good idea to move anything," said Smitty nervously.

"Didn't you ever play soldier when you were a kid?" asked Joe. Mimicking himself as a child, he crouched behind the table for a second, then popped up and pretended to shoot at Smitty. "Bang, bang!"

Forgetting where he was for a moment, Smitty reacted to the old childhood game. Clutching his chest, he yelled, "I'm hit!" But when he dramatically stumbled backward, his foot hit the leg of a small table, knocking a metal helmet from its stand. The helmet clattered noisily onto the cement floor.

Smitty and Joe froze, listening to hear if they'd been discovered. But still they didn't hear anything. Breathing a sigh of relief, Smitty picked up the helmet and put it back on its stand.

Joe placed the rifle on the table and picked up a little olive green object. It looked like a paperback book open to the middle. "Here's some reading material for you," he said as he flipped the object toward Smitty.

"Careful!" hissed Smitty, grabbing onto the object. Frowning at Joe, he carefully placed it back on the table. "I think we'd better go now," said Smitty, glancing at the stairs.

"Okay, in just a minute. I want to look at *everything*. What is that thing over there?" asked Joe.

"Those are Claymore mines," said Smitty. "You detonate them with a remote control or trip wire."

Joe looked surprised. "I'll be darned. Where'd you learn so much about weapons?" he asked.

Smitty's eyes danced with mischief. "Everyone knows country boys are born with a shotgun in their hands. I got my first squirrel by the time I was ten."

"*Right!* Which explains why you would know so much about Claymores and trip wires. They always come in handy when you're squirrel hunting," said Joe, trying not to laugh. He knew Smitty was teasing him, getting him back for all the times he'd bragged about his life in the city. "Seriously, where did you learn about this stuff?"

Smitty reached into the back pocket of his jeans and pulled out the book he'd been reading at the station. "Books," he said.

Joe shook his head in disbelief. Then he picked up a pistol, checking the chamber. It was empty. He snapped it shut. "This is cool, man. It's the kind of gun detectives use in the movies." Holding the gun against the side of his leg, he spun around toward the stairs, whipping up the shiny pistol into firing position.

He froze. Instead of an imaginary enemy, he found himself staring down the barrel of a rifle. And somehow he sensed that the rifle pointed at his chest was loaded with real bullets.

"You boys having fun down here?"

asked Mr. Johnson. The smile on his lips didn't reach his eyes. Those eyes were as hard and cold as stones in a river.

Chapter 4

Johnson looked like he'd just returned from a military inspection in his crisply-pressed fatigues and polished boots. He glared at Joe. "That weapon, boy, is a .357 Magnum," he snarled. "It is not a toy."

"No. Yes, I mean, you're right, sir. It's not a toy, sir," said Joe nervously. He lowered the gun and quickly replaced it on the table.

Johnson stepped to the table and moved the gun back to the exact spot where it had been earlier. Then Joe watched Johnson line up each weapon in a precise vertical line. He glanced at Smitty, hoping to catch his eye, but Smitty's attention was focused on the rifle in Johnson's hand.

When he seemed satisfied that his weapons were all in place, Johnson looked back at them. "I could shoot you both for trespassing, you know."

"Mr. Johnson, sir. Ah, we came out to deliver your part. But when you didn't answer the door . . . we saw a light and thought maybe you didn't hear us and so we, uh . . ." Smitty's voice trailed off. He hung his head and stared at the floor.

"We didn't mean any harm, sir," Joe said quickly, taking the package containing the cycle part from his pocket. With a weak smile, he handed the package to Johnson.

Johnson put down his rifle and opened the package. For several seconds, he examined the cycle part.

Finally, he looked at them and grinned. "I've been waiting a long time for this part. Guess I should thank you for bringing it out here."

Surprised and relieved by the

apparent change in Johnson's attitude, Joe relaxed. He threw Smitty a look that said "I told you so," but the frown on Smitty's face deepened. "So, Mr. Johnson, how long have you been collecting weapons?" asked Joe, in an attempt to be friendly.

"Long enough," answered Johnson.

"Well, you sure do have a fine collection," said Joe.

"It's important to be prepared. Only those who are prepared will survive an enemy attack," said Johnson.

"Right!" Joe agreed. *This man is a real nut case,* he thought to himself.

"One of the first rules of war is to be prepared." Johnson went on. "You let your guard down for one minute, and that's when the enemy will strike."

"Well, you sure are prepared," Joe said again, glancing around the room.

"See this weapon here?" said Johnson, pointing to a large gun. "This is an M-79. It fires grenade shells. And that one over there is an M-60—best little machine gun I ever used. It's heavy, but it gets the job done. Either of you boys ever fire a machine gun?"

"No," said Joe and Smitty, nervously answering at once.

Amusement flicked across Johnson's face. He looked like he'd just thought of something.

"But I'd sure *like* to," said Joe quickly. He didn't want to fire the machine gun, but something told him he should play along. Better to humor the crazy old guy.

"How about you? You ever fire a machine gun?" asked Johnson, turning to Smitty.

"No, but I've fired a rifle and shotgun. I *love* guns," Smitty lied.

"That so? And are you prepared to fight the enemy when they come?" growled Johnson, leaning his face just inches from Smitty's.

Smitty blinked. Johnson was so close,

he could count the wrinkles around the man's eyes and smell his aftershave. Frightened by the man's sudden change of mood, Smitty stepped back from Johnson's hard stare.

Johnson's finger snaked out and stabbed at Smitty's chest. "Answer me, boy! Are you *prepared*?" barked Johnson, sounding just like a Marine drill sergeant.

"No. I guess not." Smitty glanced nervously at Joe and then back at Johnson.

"You *want* to be prepared, don't you?" Johnson barked.

"Oh, yes. Yes, we do," lied Joe, trying to help his cousin. "In fact, just yesterday we were talking about what we would do about it if someone invaded this country."

"And I said that we really need to . . . learn how to defend ourselves," Smitty added.

"*Good!* Then you've come to the

right place! I could use some recruits."
Johnson smiled broadly at them, then
started arming himself with weapons.
He picked up two belts of linked ammo
and crisscrossed them over his chest.
Then he slung the M-60 over his
shoulder and picked up a rifle.

When Johnson wasn't looking, Joe
turned to Smitty. Exaggerating his lip
movement, he silently mouthed the
words, "What should we do now?"
Smitty's eyes darted from Johnson to
the stairs and back to Johnson. As
Smitty started to mouth the word *stairs,*
Johnson glanced over at him. Smitty
coughed and covered his mouth with
his hand.

"I sure could use a drink of water,
Mr. Johnson," said Smitty, faking
another cough.

Johnson nodded toward the stairs.
"Help yourself. The glasses are next to
the sink."

"I think I'll get a drink, too," Joe

chimed in. "Somebody just mentions water and I get thirsty. I don't know what it is. Power of suggestion, I guess. Even when I was a kid if someone started talking about having a drink of water, it made me want one, too." Johnson eyed him suspiciously. Joe smiled and shrugged his shoulders.

"Go on. It's going to be a long night." Johnson bent down and started rummaging in a box of supplies. Joe was almost to the stairs when Johnson stopped him. "Fill this up. We won't be coming back to the house every time you girls need a drink," sneered Johnson. He tossed Joe a canteen.

Joe laughed nervously. "Great." He waved the canteen in the air. Forcing himself not to run, he walked slowly up the stairs. Smitty was waiting for him by the kitchen sink. Water gushed from the faucet in a steady stream and splashed noisily down the drain.

"Let's get out of here," whispered

Smitty desperately.

"Go! I'm right behind you." Joe left the canteen on the counter and hurried after Smitty.

Once outside, they ran as fast as they could to Joe's bike. Joe turned the bike around and motioned for Smitty to jump on. Joe didn't want to take a chance on starting the engine. He didn't want Johnson to know they were leaving until it was too late for him to do anything. Silently, they coasted down the drive.

As they neared the gate, Smitty jumped off the bike and ran to open it. But just as he started to lift the latch, floodlights went on all over the yard, turning the night into day. Smitty and Joe froze in their tracks like two rabbits caught in the glaring headlights of an oncoming car.

"Going somewhere, boys?" snarled Johnson. The big man stood on the porch, holding his M-16 rifle. But now the rifle had a bayonet attached to its muzzle.

Chapter 5

A light breeze had come up, chilling the summer night. Joe shivered and wrapped his arms across his chest. But it wasn't the cold that had made him shiver—it was fear. Pure terror was racing through his body, weakening his legs and churning in his stomach. The crazed look on Johnson's face and the way the man kept waving his rifle around had turned Joe into a human jellyfish.

Joe glanced at Smitty. He looked like he was plenty scared, too. He hadn't moved an inch from the gate. His hand was still on the latch.

Johnson walked slowly down the driveway toward Joe. "You, boy! Come on up here by your friend," Johnson said, motioning for Smitty to leave the gate and join them.

"Yes, sir," said Smitty.

"Fine. That's what I like. A boy who can take orders," said Johnson. He smiled at them. "Now both of you move away from that bike." He swung his gun to the left and pointed to a spot near the house.

Joe glanced at Smitty, but his cousin just shrugged.

"I said, MOVE IT!" ordered Johnson.

They both jumped at the harshness in Johnson's voice. They almost ran to the place where Johnson was pointing.

"I guess I had you girls figured all wrong. For a minute there, I thought you were on my side," said Johnson quietly.

"But we *are*," said Smitty, softly. "Tell him, Joe."

"Yeah!" Joe flashed a big smile at Johnson, hoping to convince the older man. Johnson stared at them without blinking. He seemed to have flipped back into another time zone, another place. Johnson's strange trancelike stare made Joe uneasy. "We just thought we'd come back on another night when Smitty felt better and . . ."

"Lies! The enemy will say anything to make you believe him. They will pretend to be friendly, but they're too dumb to know that you're fighting the war to help them. It's a mistake to trust them, because one day you might wake up and find them standing over you with a knife—ready to cut your throat," said Johnson, breathing heavily. His mind was definitely somewhere else, lost in the jungle of his past.

"No, *really!* We're your friends. We're on your side," said Smitty.

Johnson seemed to snap back into the present. "You had me fooled back there," Johnson said, indicating the house. "I guess I've been out of action too long. But we can remedy that, can't we boys?" Johnson's face twisted with a cruel, insane-looking smile.

"Look—we're sorry, sir. We didn't mean to run off. We really do want you to teach us—help us get prepared and all," said Joe. He knew he was babbling, but he couldn't help it.

"Oh, I'm going to *teach* you all right," chuckled Johnson, raising his weapon. "And one of the first rules of war is to immobilize the enemy." Johnson walked over to Joe's bike. He kicked the front tire of the cycle with his boot. Then, grinning at Joe, he thrust the blade of his bayonet deep into the tire.

Without thinking, Joe ran toward Johnson. Anger pumped through his body. "What do you think you're doing?" Joe screamed.

Whirling around, Johnson aimed his gun at Joe's stomach. "Stop right there, boy!"

Johnson's warning quickly brought Joe to a standstill. Now he could feel his anger giving way to fear again.

Walking to the back of the bike, Johnson slashed the other tire. Joe heard the hissing of the escaping air. Again, his anger overwhelmed him. "You're going to *pay* for those tires!" he threatened.

The smile on Mr. Johnson's face disappeared. He started toward Joe.

"Look, he didn't mean it, okay?" Smitty spluttered. "We just want to go home, Mr. Johnson."

"Shut up! You are both a couple of babies. You come out here, snoop around, and when the going gets tough, you want to go home," sneered Johnson. "You think the enemy lets you go free when you don't want to fight anymore? You think the army cares if you're sick and tired and want to go home? No. No one cares about you in war. Now get going." He waved his rifle in the direction of the mountains. "I'll give you a five-minute head start just to make this interesting."

"But town is that way," said Smitty, pointing in the opposite direction.

"The clock is running, mister," barked Johnson. He fired a burst of bullets at the ground near their feet.

Smitty jumped up in a flash. "Come on, Joe. Let's go!"

Joe glanced back at his bike. Lying on its side with its tires flat, it looked like a giant dead beetle. He could also see that the front fender was bent. Until tonight there hadn't been any dings or scratches on the bike. He felt like crying. Sure, the bike could be repaired, but it would never be brand new again. He shot Johnson a look of pure hatred, wondering if he could charge the older man and beat him up. Johnson smirked. It was as if he could read Joe's mind. He pointed the gun at Joe's chest.

"Come on, Joe! Please, let's go,"

Smitty pleaded desperately.

"You have four minutes," snarled Johnson, punctuating his words with another burst of bullets near their feet.

The bullets kicked up the dirt in front of Joe's boots. He jumped and turned to Smitty. Together, they started running across the clearing toward the dark, forbidding mountains. When Joe glanced back in Johnson's direction, he was surprised to see that the older man had disappeared.

Reaching the edge of the clearing, the boys plunged into the trees. The woods were dark and overgrown. "Smitty, do you know these woods?" Joe asked, breathlessly.

"No," Smitty called back as he ran wildly forward in the darkness.

"Well, what are we going to do, man?" hissed Joe, trying to catch up with his long-legged cousin.

"I don't know. Find a place to hide, I guess."

Suddenly, the quiet exploded with the loud, popping sounds of gunfire. Flashes of red illuminated the darkness as round after round of ammunition flew through the air. Bullets ripped the bark from the trees. Joe screamed and fell to the ground. Smitty scrambled for cover behind a fallen log.

Chapter 6

As suddenly as the gunfire had started, it stopped. Silence settled over the woods like a feather comforter. Pine needles floated down from a nearby tree and landed on Joe's cheek. He didn't brush them away. He didn't want to move. He wanted to stay there forever, hugging the ground, where he felt safe. Tears streamed from his eyes. He was scared. He didn't want to die.

Smitty crawled out from behind the fallen log and inched his way to Joe. "You okay?" he whispered softly.

"Yeah," said Joe.

"We gotta get out of here. Johnson is sure to find us soon."

"I don't know how he got up here so fast," said Joe, sitting up. He drew the back of his hand across his eyes, streaking the tears and dirt on his face.

"We gotta go. Stay close and keep quiet," Smitty instructed as he started off through the trees. Smitty glided through the woods like a ghost, disappearing and reappearing farther on ahead.

Joe followed, but he wasn't nearly as quiet as Smitty. He winced every time he accidentally stepped on a twig or branch. The cracking noise of wood breaking underfoot sounded like thunderclaps in his ears. He worried that Johnson had heard him. He was about six tree-lengths from Smitty when Johnson fired another round into the woods. Instead of taking cover, Joe started to run. Crashing noisily through the brush, he passed Smitty.

"Get down!" yelled Smitty.

Joe didn't listen. He kept going. Tracer flashes lit up the woods. Joe liked the light. It made it easier for him to see what lay ahead. Then, suddenly, he felt his legs being pulled out from under him. He tumbled forward.

"Sorry," Smitty said, apologizing for having tackled him. "He wasn't firing at us. Those are tracer rounds. He's trying to get a fix on our position. And you're helping him."

"What are we going to do? Just lie here until he finds us? I know we can outrun him, man," said Joe, spitting dirt from his mouth.

"That's just what he wants us to do. Don't you see that we're playing his game? He knows we're scared. He knows we'll run like rabbits every time he fires," explained Smitty.

"So what do we do?"

"Outsmart him!"

"What?" asked Joe.

"We have to think like he does if we want to beat him at his own game."

"Oh, that'll be easy—think like a wacko," Joe said sarcastically. But the minute the words left his mouth, he regretted them. It wasn't his cousin's fault that they were in this mess.

Smitty ignored Joe's remark. "We know he's waiting for us to show ourselves. He knows we'll run whenever he fires a tracer round, so what do we do? We hide and . . ."

Joe interrupted Smitty in mid-sentence. "Try to figure out where he is. Then we jump him."

"No—he would expect that. We circle around behind him and hightail it back to the house," said Smitty.

Another tracer round lit up the woods. The boys tensed, but as agreed, they didn't move. A few seconds later, Smitty silently motioned for Joe to follow him. Keeping their bodies close to the ground, they worked their way to an area overgrown with bushes and brush. Carefully, they crawled under the bushes. Hoping the leaves would camouflage their position, they waited.

Joe didn't hear Johnson until he was almost on top of them. He held his breath and glanced out of the corner of his eye at Smitty. His cousin's face was rigid with control. Joe forced himself to look back toward Johnson. The man, he could see, had turned and was staring in their direction. Joe wanted to duck farther down into the bushes, but he knew that even the slightest movement on his part would give away their position.

Johnson reached into his pocket and took out a grenade. Slowly, he pulled out the firing pin. Holding the release clamp of the grenade securely with his finger, he peered into the bushy area where Smitty and Joe were hidden.

Joe didn't dare look at Smitty. He guessed his cousin was feeling as scared as he was. Beads of sweat rolled down Joe's forehead, and his heart was beating faster than the drum beat in a heavy-metal song. *Please, dear God*, he prayed, *don't let him see us.*

Johnson stepped closer to the bushes. He leaned forward and studied the shape of the shrubbery. Then something moved behind him in the forest, disturbing the silence. Johnson spun around and threw the grenade. A deafening boom filled the air as the grenade exploded in a burst of fire.

The sound of the exploding grenade echoed in Joe's ears. He rolled his eyes toward Smitty, but his cousin's eyes were squeezed shut. He looked like a person bracing himself for a jolt of expected pain.

Joe wanted to reach out and touch his cousin's arm and reassure him. But he couldn't—Johnson was only a few feet away. Joe studied Johnson's back and considered the possibility of rushing the deranged old man.

Chapter 7

Joe was about to tackle Johnson from behind when the man walked off in the opposite direction. Joe imagined Johnson proudly inspecting the part of the woods he had just blown to smithereens. Again, his anger started to bubble to the surface. But then he chided himself for not jumping on Johnson when he had had the chance. Lost in his own thoughts, he jumped when Smitty touched his arm.

Holding his finger to his lips, Smitty motioned for Joe to follow. Slowly, quietly, Smitty glided through the bushes, stopping every so often to look around. Joe followed, stopping when Smitty stopped and moving forward when Smitty moved. For the first time that night, he realized that he was moving through the woods without making a sound. He had picked up Smitty's rhythm, soft and quick.

Soon they were trotting down the mountain, zigzagging around, dodging branches and ducking under low-hanging limbs. Once in a while, Joe glanced over his shoulder for signs of Johnson. When he didn't see him, he felt a rush of relief.

Then the boys stopped to catch their breath. "So what are we going to do now?" Joe whispered.

"First, we have to make it across that field," answered Smitty. Floodlights lit up the clearing like a football field during a big game. "If he's anywhere near here, though, he's going to see us when we run across. He'll pick us off like sitting ducks."

"I don't plan to be sitting," said Joe. "In fact, I plan to run across that field faster than I've ever run in my life."

Smitty chuckled. "Faster than a speeding bullet?"

"Faster than the speed of light, cuz," said Joe, cracking a smile. "Who knows—maybe the General is still climbing the mountain."

"I wouldn't count on it," answered Smitty, the grin fading from his face. "We'd better get moving now."

"Okay," said Joe, taking a deep breath. "Ready, set, go!"

Together, they broke from the treeline, running as fast as they could. They ran straight toward their goal—Johnson's house. Propelled by fear, they both ran faster than they ever thought they could.

Smitty reached the back of the house first, with Joe following close on his heels. As he caught his breath, Joe spotted Johnson's Harley parked a few feet away. "That's it!" he cried. Jumping with excitement, he grabbed Smitty by the shoulders and spun him around.

"What?" asked Smitty.

"Johnson's bike! We can ride it out of here," said Joe, dashing toward the big bike.

"Can you get it started?" asked Smitty excitedly.

"Yeah, I think so," answered Joe, studying the buttons on the bike's handlebars. He pressed the starter button. Nothing happened. He looked up from the bike and saw Smitty busily opening and closing the cupboard doors that lined the back wall of the house. "Smitty, what are you doing?"

"I'm looking for the fuse box," said Smitty. Opening the last of the old wooden cupboards, he whooped with delight. *"Gotcha!"* Smitty quickly began to unscrew the fuses from the box. As he removed the last one, the floodlights on the house and the field went out. Smitty hurried over to Joe. "Now we'll have a much better chance of getting away in the dark."

"Good idea," said Joe, without looking up. When he was finished hotwiring the bike, he cranked the throttle. The engine turned over twice, then died. Frustrated, Joe slammed his fist against the bike's handlebars.

"What happened?" asked Smitty.

"I flooded the engine. We're going to have to wait a minute," said Joe. He stared off in the darkness toward the mountains. "Smitty, what if he gets to the gate before we do?"

"Well, I hadn't thought about that," admitted Smitty.

Suddenly, the quiet of the night was shattered by the sound of gunfire. Joe glanced at his cousin and then started pushing the bike forward. "Help me, Smitty! We've got to get this bike into the barn."

Chapter 8

The wooden floor groaned with the weight of the heavy cycle as Joe and Smitty pushed the Harley into the barn. It was dark inside, darker than the moonless night outside. High up above, in the rafters, they heard the flapping and rustling of wings.

"What's that noise?" asked Joe. He squinted up at the ceiling, but it was too dark to see anything.

"Probably bats," answered Smitty.

Joe shivered. He hated things that went bump in the night. He wanted to run back outside. But he would have to put up with the bats if it meant escaping Johnson. He hunched his shoulders up near his ears, hoping to protect his neck. Somewhere he'd heard that bats like to attack the neck—especially vampire bats.

Smitty saw Joe staring at the ceiling. His body was so scrunched up that his neck seemed to have disappeared. "Forget the bats, man."

Joe was tired. He had never faced so many dangers in one night. It was like being trapped in a chamber of horrors. He took a deep, slow breath to calm his jittery nerves.

"Okay, okay! Jeez, it's dark in here," said Joe. He reached into his jeans and pulled out a butane lighter.

"I thought you quit smoking," said Smitty, looking surprised.

"I did. I just carry this as a souvenir of a bad habit," said Joe truthfully. He flicked his lighter. Together, the boys looked around the barn. Smitty spotted Johnson's toolbox and several ropes next to some sacks of grain. He bent down and rummaged in the box.

Turning to Joe, he handed him a

wire cutter. "Get me some wire from those hay bales." Then he grabbed a coil of rope and started tying one end to the bottom of a wooden post.

"Okay, here's the wire," said Joe, curiously. "Now what?"

"Now take off your shirt," Smitty ordered as he secured the rope.

"My *shirt?*"

"Hurry up and stuff it with hay," instructed Smitty.

"A *dummy?* Is that your plan?" asked Joe, finally catching the drift of Smitty's thinking.

"Yes. First we tie the dummy on the bike. Then, when Johnson comes in here thinking that he's got us, we jump on him."

"I don't know. What if he . . ."

"What if he *what?* If you've got a better plan, let's hear it," Smitty snapped. He carefully stretched the rope across the floor in front of the bike's front wheel.

"There, I think this will work," Smitty said, straightening up and taking off his jeans.

"Now that I know what I'm doing, I'm sure I can get the engine to turn over this time. Johnson has really kept this old baby in great shape," said Joe as he helped Smitty finish wiring the dummy to the bike seat.

"We need a head," said Smitty. Seeing a bunch of rags in the corner, he got an idea. "I'll make it."

Suddenly, Johnson's voice broke the stillness of the night. "All right, you girls! I know you're in here somewhere. Just come out with your hands up."

Joe and Smitty froze. "Give me that head," whispered Joe. Smitty jammed a big handful of straw into a rag and handed it to Joe.

"Hurry!" whispered Smitty. He held the stuffed head upright while Joe wrapped the wire.

"If you surrender now, I'll treat you

fairly. You'll be accorded the rights of all prisoners of war—just like it says in the rules of the Geneva Convention," yelled Johnson. Then he laughed. The terrible sound of Johnson's laugh sent chills down Joe's back. He didn't believe a word. The man was insane.

"Start the bike, then come over here with me," whispered Smitty, hiding behind a stack of hay bales. In his hand, he held the end of the rope.

Joe pressed the Harley's starter. The bike's engine roared to life, filling the barn with a deafening growl. "I hope this works," said Joe, crouching down next to Smitty.

Smitty took a deep breath and exhaled. "When he trips over this rope, we jump him, get his gun, and then tie him up, okay?"

"Okay." Joe didn't want to think about what might happen if their trick didn't work. He glanced sideways at his cousin. Smitty looked tense, his eyes glued on the open barn door. Both boys silently rehearsed their parts. Smitty would pull the rope, tripping Johnson and making him fall. Once he was down, Joe would jump on him.

Then Johnson entered the barn. "All right, girls. Get off the Harley," the man sneered as he headed for the bike.

When Johnson reached the Harley's front wheel, Smitty tightened the rope and yelled, "*Now!*"

As Johnson tripped, Joe leaped up and over the bales of hay and threw himself down on the groaning man. Johnson struggled to free himself, but Joe stayed glued to his back. Smitty grabbed the rifle and stepped back. "It's over, Johnson!" he shouted.

Joe rolled free of the older man and grabbed a short piece of rope. He quickly tied Johnson's hands behind his back. Then he shoved him down into a loose pile of hay. Johnson's body sagged in defeat. His mind flipped into another time, another place, where only the reciting of his name, rank, and serial number mattered.

Joe looked at Johnson and shook his head sadly. The General must have lost it a long, long time ago.

"Take the Harley into town, Joe. Get us some help. I'll stay here and watch Johnson," said Smitty.

Joe nodded. It had been a long and terrifying night—a night he wouldn't forget as long as he lived. Pulling the dummy off the bike, he climbed on.

For a moment, Joe just sat there. He looked at Smitty and smiled. "You know, cuz, you are about the baddest dude I know." Then he released the brake, and the Harley thundered out of the barn into the dawn of a new day.